Disney's

Donald Duck Stories

Including *Donald Duck and the One Bear, Donald Duck's Toy Sailboat, Donald Duck: Some Ducks Have All the Luck*

A GOLDEN BOOK • NEW YORK
Western Publishing Company, Inc., Racine, Wisconsin 53404

 Library of Congress Catalog Card Number: 89-82143
ISBN: 0-307-15829-2/ISBN: 0-307-65849-X (lib. bdg.) MCMXCII

Donald Duck and the One Bear

Donald Duck was taking something out of the oven when his three nephews walked into the kitchen.

"Those pizzas sure look good," said Huey.

"Two of them do, anyway," added Dewey.

"What's that *other* one?" asked Louie, wrinkling his nose.

"That's my personal favorite," said Donald as he set the pizzas on the table. "Pineapple and sardines. And there's a pizza with pepperoni on it for Daisy and one with sausage for you boys."

"Yummy!" chorused the boys, reaching for their pizza.

"Don't touch!" scolded Donald. "Let me cut them. We'll go get Daisy first, and the pizzas will be just cool enough to eat when we get back."

No sooner had they left than a big brown bear came down the street. When he got to Donald's house, he stopped. He sniffed and sniffed. Something smelled good!

The bear lumbered up the sidewalk to the kitchen window and looked in. When he saw the pizzas sitting on the table, he gave a happy little growl and crawled right through the open window.

The bear tried to pick up a piece of Daisy's pepperoni pizza, but it was too hot. He picked up a piece of the boys' sausage pizza and took a bite, but it was too cold. Then he tried Donald's pineapple and sardine pizza, and it was just right. He ate one piece after another, until it was all gone.

With his tummy full of pizza, the bear looked around for a place to rest. He wandered into the living room and sat down on the couch, where Huey, Dewey, and Louie always watched TV. The couch was too soft.

Then he tried the chair where Daisy sat when she came to visit. He didn't sit there very long. Daisy had left her knitting—with the needles in it!

At last he sat down in Donald's favorite rocker. That was just right. He rocked, and he rocked harder, and he rocked harder still, until—CRASH!—the chair suddenly tipped over backward and the bear spilled onto the floor.

Grumbling to himself, the bear lumbered upstairs. He wanted to sleep on something that didn't move! So first he tried Huey's bed, but it was too small.

Then he tried stretching across from Dewey's bed to Louie's, but he sagged in the middle.

Finally he found Donald's bed, and that was just right! He snuggled down into the covers and fell fast asleep.

When Donald, Daisy, and the boys came back, Donald proudly pointed to the pizzas. But Daisy could only cry, "Somebody's been trying to eat my pizza!"

"Somebody's been eating *our* pizza!" exclaimed the boys. "Look! There's a bite out of this piece!"

"Hey!" shouted Donald. "Somebody's been eating *my* pizza—and has eaten it all up! I'm going to get to the bottom of this!" He stormed off to the living room, with Daisy and the boys following nervously.

"I can't believe there are *two* people in the world who like pineapple and sardine pizza," Dewey whispered to his brothers. Then he stopped and pointed. "Look!"

Huey and Louie were amazed. "Somebody's been sitting on our couch!" said Huey.

"And squashed the cushions!" added Louie.

"Somebody's been sitting in my chair," said Daisy, holding up a broken knitting needle.

"My rocker!" yelled Donald. "Somebody sat in my rocker and broke it to pieces!"

Daisy and the boys tried to tell Donald that his chair was just tipped over, not broken, but he was too angry to listen. He charged up the stairs two at a time. Daisy and the boys tagged along.

"Hey!" shouted Huey, pausing in the doorway of the boys' room. "Somebody's been sleeping in my bed!"

"And my bed!" added Dewey.

"Mine too!" said Louie.

"Help!" screamed Donald from his room.

The boys ran down the hall and found Donald hiding behind the dresser.

"Here's the culprit," Daisy told the boys, laughing.

"A bear!" said Huey.

"He's cute!" added Dewey.

"Can we keep him, Uncle Donald?" asked Louie.

Donald poked his head out from behind the dresser. Seeing the boys and Daisy standing nearby and the bear still sleeping soundly, he tried to act brave. "C-Certainly n-not," he said. "We have to wake the bear and get him downstairs and out of the house right away and—"

The doorbell rang. "I'll get it!" Donald shouted, leaping out of the room.

A worried-looking little man stood at the door. "I'm sorry to bother you," he said, "but I don't know what's happened to my Pizza—"

"We've been wondering that ourselves," Donald interrupted. "Mine got eaten all up, and—"

"No, no, no, no!" the man said frantically. "Pizza is my pet bear! You see, I own Charlie's Pizza, and our slogan is 'When you're as hungry as a bear, eat Charlie's Pizza.' Get it?"

"I get it," Donald said. "But I'd be happier if *you'd* get your *bear*. He's upstairs."

The man ran upstairs yelling, "Pizza! Pizza!"

The bear woke up when he heard the man's voice and greeted him affectionately. Charlie snapped a leash to Pizza's collar, and the bear followed him down the stairs and out the door.

"Whew!" breathed Donald. "I'm glad that's over!"
"It was kinda exciting, though," said Huey.
"Let's eat!" said Dewey.
"Yuck! Cold pizza," said Louie.

Just then the doorbell rang again. It was Charlie, holding three big boxes.

"I want to give you this reward for finding my bear," he said. "Three piping-hot, extra-large pizzas."

"Hurray!" the boys cheered.

"How very kind!" said Daisy.

"I hope you like them," Charlie added. "They're Pizza's favorite—pineapple and sardines. Thanks again for finding him!"

Huey, Dewey, Louie, and Daisy stared glumly at the pizzas, but Donald grinned from ear to ear. "I liked that bear from the moment I saw him," he said. "Now, let's eat!"

Donald Duck's Toy Sailboat

"There!" said Donald Duck. "At last it's done!"

He stood back to look at his toy sailboat. Making it had been a big job. It had taken him all summer long. But now the boat was finished, and it was beautiful.

The mantel was just the place for it, too. The whole room looked better with the sailboat up there.

"Building sailboats is hungry work," Donald said to himself. So he fixed himself a fine big lunch.

"Now to try out the boat in the lake," he thought. But his hard work had made him sleepy, too. So Donald settled down for a nap after lunch. He would try out the boat later.

Outside Donald's cottage, in the old elm tree, lived two little chipmunks, Chip and Dale. And they had had no lunch at all.

"I'm hungry," said Chip, rubbing his empty middle.

"Me too," said Dale. But suddenly he brightened. "Look!" he said.

Chip looked and looked. At last he spied it—one lone acorn still clinging to the bough of an oak tree down beside the lake.

Down the elm tree they raced, across to the oak, and up its rough-barked trunk.

"Mine!" cried Chip, reaching for the nut.

"I saw it first!" Dale cried.

So they pushed and they tugged and they tussled, until the acorn slipped through their fingers and fell—*kerplunk*—into the lake.

The two little chipmunks looked mighty sad as they watched the acorn float away. But Dale soon brightened. "Look!" he cried.

Chip looked. On a little island out in the middle of the lake stood a great big oak tree weighted down with acorns on every side.

Down to the shore the chipmunks ran. But br-r-r! It was too cold to swim.

"How can we get to them?" wondered Chip.

"I don't know," said Dale. But he soon had an idea. "Look in there!" he said.

They could see the toy sailboat on the mantel in Donald Duck's cottage.

"Come on," said Dale. So away they raced, straight in the cottage door.

They had the sailboat down and almost out the door when Donald stirred in his sleep.

"Nice day for a sail," he said dreamily as the boat slipped smoothly past him.

Soon after, Donald woke up completely.

"Now to try out my boat!" he cried.

Suddenly something outside the window caught his eye. It was his sailboat, out on the lake! And in it were Chip and Dale!

"I'll fix those chipmunks!" Donald said.

He pulled out his rod and reel and chose a painted fishing lure. It looked just like a nut.

"This will do," Donald said with a grin.

From the pier, he cast that little fishing lure as far as he could. With a *plop* it landed beside the toy boat.

"Look! Look at this!" cried Dale. He leaned way over the edge of the boat to pull in the floating lure.

"Good! A nut!" said Chip. "We'll toss it in the hold and have it for supper tonight."

As soon as it was fast in the hold, Donald pulled in the line. He pulled the little boat right in to shore. The chipmunks never suspected a thing. They did not even notice Donald pouring water into the cabin of the boat.

Chip discovered that when he went into the cabin. "Man the pumps!" he cried.

The two chipmunks worked with might and main while Donald watched and laughed.

"Ha ha!" chuckled Donald. The chipmunks looked up.

"So that's the trouble!" Dale cried.

He pulled the fishing lure from the hold and flung it at Donald so that he was soon tangled up in fishing line.

Before Donald could free himself, the chipmunks set sail once more.

By the time Donald launched his swift canoe, the chipmunks had touched at the island's shore.

As Donald was paddling briskly along, he heard a brisk *rat-a-tat-tat*!

The oak tree on the island seemed to shiver and shake as acorns rained down.

The busy little chipmunks finished dancing on the branches. Then they hauled their harvest on board.

"Oh, well," said Donald, watching from his canoe. "At least I know the sailboat really will sail. Now let's just see what those little fellows do."

And can you guess what the chipmunks did? They stored their nuts in a hollow tree. And they took Donald's toy sailboat and put it right back where it belonged!

Donald Duck
Some Ducks Have All the Luck

Donald Duck was pacing the floor.
"Uncle Donald..." said Huey.
"What's wrong?" asked Dewey.
"You're making us dizzy!" cried Louie.
"Today is Daisy's birthday," declared Donald, "and I need to get her a better present than Gladstone Gander."

"That's easy, Uncle Donald," said Huey.

"Just get Daisy a bigger, fancier present than he does," said Dewey.

"But Gladstone's so lucky, and I'm broke," Donald complained. "He'll probably buy Daisy something expensive. And besides, how can I buy something better when I don't even know what he's giving her?"

Just then Donald glanced out the window and noticed someone walking down the street.

"Gladstone Gander!" he exclaimed. "Maybe it's my lucky day after all. I'll follow him all over town until I see what he's buying for Daisy."

Gladstone Gander was worrying, too.

"I sure hope I get lucky today. I have to come up with a really great present for Daisy," he thought as he walked along.

"Ah, this must be my good luck now!" Gladstone exclaimed when he saw some money lying on the sidewalk. But it was only a one-dollar bill.

"Every little bit helps," Gladstone said with a sigh as he put the bill in his pocket.

Gladstone stopped at a jewelry store and looked in the window.

He chuckled when he recognized Donald's reflection in the store window.

"I bet Donald is following me," thought Gladstone. "He is as worried about Daisy's present as I am. I know how to give him a real scare."

Gladstone Gander marched into the jewelry store and looked at some diamond bracelets. He held them up, just to make sure Donald saw.

Outside, poor Donald Duck groaned. "That must have been a thousand-dollar bill he just found! Now he's buying Daisy a diamond bracelet. Some ducks have all the luck!" Donald thought.

Gladstone's next stop was the Bonbon Boutique, which sold the most expensive chocolates in Duckburg.

Donald went into the store after Gladstone came out. He almost fainted when the clerk told him the price of one 14-karat chocolate bonbon.

Donald caught up with Gladstone Gander outside the Sniff of Success Perfume Shop. Gladstone couldn't resist teasing Donald.

"Fancy meeting you here, Donald. I was just trying to decide what to give Daisy for her birthday—a diamond bracelet, a 100-karat chocolate bonbon, or a bottle of Liquid Gold, 'The Perfume Too Expensive to Wear,'" said Gladstone gleefully.

Donald was overwhelmed. He slunk away.

Gladstone Gander enjoyed his laugh. But soon he remembered that he still had no present for Daisy and only one dollar in his pocket.

"I need some good luck, and I need it now!" thought Gladstone as he hurried home.

"Hello, Mr. Gander," said the mail carrier. "I just left a special-delivery letter in your mailbox."

"Maybe I've won another contest," Gladstone thought as he tore open the envelope. He read eagerly, "You have been selected to receive dinner for two at the grand opening of Chez Swann, the swankiest restaurant in Duckburg."

Gladstone whooped. "My good luck strikes again! This is the perfect present for Daisy. Donald doesn't have a chance."

Meanwhile, a sad Donald Duck was climbing the steps of his house.

"We have a surprise for you, Uncle Donald," said Huey, Dewey, and Louie.

"I'm not interested in surprises," Donald moaned.

"But we found out what Aunt Daisy wants most for her birthday, and we got it for you," said Huey.

"The present is all wrapped up and waiting in the car," added Dewey.

"So let's go!" shouted Louie, racing for the car.

Donald and his nephews had been at Daisy's house for a little while when a knock came at the door. It was Gladstone Gander.

"Happy birthday, dear Daisy!" Gladstone exclaimed. "How would you like to go to the opening night of Chez Swann, the swankiest restaurant in Duckburg?"

"I'd love to, Gladstone," Daisy replied. "But I simply can't leave my darling kitty that Donald gave me," she added, cuddling the tiny kitten until it purred and purred and purrrrred.

"I have an idea! Why don't you and Donald have my birthday dinner together? You can sing 'Happy Birthday' to me," Daisy said, showing them both to the door.

Donald Duck had a great time at Chez Swann. He lifted his glass and toasted, "To Daisy and her kitty!"

"To Daisy," Gladstone Gander agreed. Then he grumbled, "Some ducks have all the luck."